Wolf Island

Celia Godkin

Fitzhenry & Whiteside

W9-AWE-821

For my mother.
C.G.

Copyright © 1993 by Celia Godkin
New editions published in 2006

Published in Canada by Fitzhenry & Whiteside,
195 Allstate Parkway, Markham, Ontario L3R 4T8

Published in the United States by Fitzhenry & Whiteside,
311 Washington Street, Brighton, Massachusetts 02135

All rights reserved. No part of this book may be reproduced in any manner without the express written consent
of the publisher, except in the case of brief excerpts in critical reviews and articles. All inquiries should be addressed to
Fitzhenry & Whiteside Limited, 195 Allstate Parkway, Markham, Ontario L3R 4T8.

www.fitzhenry.ca   godwit@fitzhenry.ca

10 9 8 7 6 5 4 3 2

Library and Archives Canada Cataloguing in Publication

Godkin, Celia
Wolf island / Celia Godkin.

First published: 1989.
ISBN-13: 978-1-55455-007-4 (bound)
ISBN-10: 1-55455-007-6 (bound)
ISBN-13: 978-1-55455-008-1 (pbk.)
ISBN-10: 1-55455-008-4 (pbk.)

1. Wolves—Juvenile fiction. I. Title.

PS8563.O8185W64 2006   jC813'.54   C2006-903455-9

**U.S. Publisher Cataloging-in-Publication Data
(Library of Congress Standards)**

Godkin, Celia.
Wolf island / Celia Godkin.
Originally published: NY : Scientific American Books for Young
Readers, 1993.
[36] p. : col. ill. ; 29 cm.
Summary: Set on an island in Northern Ontario, the Wolf Island story chronicles
what happens when the highest link in the food chain is removed.
ISBN-10: 1554550076
ISBN-13: 9781554550074
ISBN-10: 1554550084 (pbk.)
ISBN-13: 9781554550081 (pbk.)
1. Island ecology — Juvenile literature. 2. Wolves — Ecology —Juvenile literature.
3. Biotic communities — Juvenile literature.
574.5/267 dc22   QH541.5.I8G63 2006

Fitzhenry & Whiteside acknowledges with thanks the Canada Council for the Arts, and the Ontario Arts Council
for their support of our publishing program. We acknowledge the financial support of the Government of Canada
through the Book Publishing Industry Development Program (BPIDP) for our publishing activities.

Canada Council   Conseil des Arts
for the Arts   du Canada

ONTARIO ARTS COUNCIL
CONSEIL DES ARTS DE L'ONTARIO

Design by Wycliffe Smith Design Inc.

Printed in Hong Kong, China by Sheck Wah Tong, June 2011, job# 54398.

Once there was an island. It was an island with trees and meadows, and many kinds of animals. There were mice, rabbits and deer, squirrels, foxes, and several kinds of birds.

All the animals on the island depended on the plants and the other animals for their food and well-being. Some animals ate grass and other plants; some ate insects; some ate other animals. The island animals were healthy. There was plenty of food for all.

A family of wolves lived on the island, too—a male wolf, a female, and their five pups.

One day, the wolf pups were playing on the beach while their mother and father slept. The pups found a strange object at the edge of the water.

It was a log raft, nailed together with boards. The pups had never seen anything like this before. They were very curious.

The wolf pups climbed onto the raft and sniffed about. Everything smelled different.

While the pups were poking around, the raft began to drift slowly out into the lake. At first the pups didn't notice anything wrong. Then, suddenly, there was nothing but water all around the raft.

The pups were scared. They howled. The mother and father wolf heard the howling and came running down to the water's edge.

The pups couldn't turn the raft back, and the pups were too scared to swim, so the adult wolves swam out to the raft and climbed aboard. The raft drifted slowly and steadily over to the mainland. Finally, it came to rest on the shore, and the wolf family scrambled onto dry land.

There were no longer any wolves on the island.

Time passed. Spring grew into summer on the island, and summer into fall. The leaves turned red. Geese flew south, and squirrels stored up nuts for the winter.

Winter was mild that year, with little snow. The green plants were buried under a thin white layer. Deer dug through the snow to find food. They had enough to eat.

The next spring, many fawns were born.

There were now many deer on the island. They were eating large amounts of grass and leaves. The wolf family had kept the deer population down, because wolves eat deer for food.

Without wolves to hunt the deer, there were now too many deer on the island for the amount of food available.

Spring grew into summer and summer into fall. More and more deer ate more and more grass and more and more leaves.

Rabbits had less to eat, because the deer were eating their food. There were not many baby bunnies born that year.

Foxes had less to eat, because there were fewer rabbits for them to hunt.

Mice had less to eat, because the deer had eaten the grass and grass seed. There were not many baby mice born that year.

Owls had less to eat, because there were fewer mice for them to hunt. Many animals on the island were hungry.

The first snow fell. Squirrels curled up in their holes, wrapped their tails around themselves for warmth, and went to sleep. The squirrels were lucky. They had collected a store of nuts for the winter.

Other animals did not have winter stores. They had to find food in the snow. Winter is a hard time for animals, but this winter was harder than most. The snow was deep and the weather cold.

Most of the plants had already been eaten during the summer and fall. Those few that remained were hard to find, buried deep under the snow.

Rabbits were hungry.
Foxes were hungry. Mice
were hungry. Owls were
hungry. Even the deer
were hungry. The whole
island was hungry.

The owls flew over to
the mainland, looking for
mice. They flew over the
wolf family walking along
the mainland shore.

The wolves were thin
and hungry, too. They had
not found a home, because
there were other wolf
families on the mainland.
The other wolves did not
want to share with them.

Snow fell for many weeks. The drifts became deeper and deeper. It was harder and harder for animals to find food. Animals grew weaker, and some began to die.

The deer were so hungry they gnawed bark from the trees. Trees began to die.

Snow covered the island. The weather grew colder and colder. Ice began to form in the water around the island and along the mainland coast. It grew thicker and thicker, spreading farther and farther out into the open water.

One day, the ice reached all the way from the mainland to the island.

The wolf family crossed the ice and returned to their old home.

The wolves were hungry
when they reached the island.
There were many weak and
sick deer for them to eat. The
wolves left the healthy deer
alone.

30

Finally, spring came. The snow melted, and grass and leaves began to grow. The wolves remained in their island home, hunting deer. No longer would there be too many deer on the island. Grass and trees would grow again. Rabbits would find enough food. The mice would find enough food. There would be food for the foxes and owls. And there would be food for the deer. The island would have food enough for all.

Life on the island was back in balance.